Little Memories
Book II

Little Memories
Book II

Anne Logan

The Pentland Press Ltd
Edinburgh   Cambridge   Durham   USA

Published by
The Pentland Press Ltd
1 Hutton Close
South Church
Bishop Auckland
Durham

ISBN : 1 85821 820 9

Typeset, printed and bound
by Lintons Printers, Crook, County Durham

To my husband and two daughters, Valerie and Sharon.
Also to Tina for all her typing skills.

CONTENTS

GENETICALLY MODIFIED

Barren land
Dry as sand
Government
Did not relent
Goods sold
No one told
Hush things up
Cover up
People ill
All is still
People used
Crops abused
Dry as twigs
Guinea pigs
No good
GM food.

LIFE IN THE OLD DOGS YET

Looking at you sitting in a chair,
Wrinkled hands, snow white hair,
Breathing gently, quite content,
Shoulders hunched, back bent.
But look closer, look inside,
Youth's still there, it doesn't hide,
When you waken up and look at me
Do you see in me what in you I see?
Handsome face and twinkling eyes,
A love, a warmth that age defies,
My heart still leaps when you hold my hand
As it supports me to help me stand.
No longer into a busy day we race
But take things at a much slower pace
We still laugh and have great fun
Getting old doesn't mean you're done,
Don't you worry, don't you fret,
There's still plenty life in these old dogs yet.

OLD TABBY CAT

I ask her to come in
And have a little chat
I make her very welcome
I'm very good at that.

She'll sit with me at dinner
And have the best of meat
Then we'll both sit down together
On a warm and comfy seat.

She is a great companion
I tell her all my woes
And when I go to sleep at night
She curls up at my toes.

She's worth every single penny
I spend on her each day
She's always waiting up for me
I know she'll never stray.

She is my very best friend
There is no doubt of that
As she looks up at me purring
My faithful old tabby cat.

THE ICICLE

Like diamonds sparkling
In the sunlight
With each movement
Shining bright.
Sun rises higher
Dazzling, dancing
Like little stars
Or fairies prancing.
Dripping starts
There's only a glimmer
The warmer it gets
Sparkles get dimmer.
The spectacle's gone
Gone, gone where?
Our icicle's melted
No longer there.

AUTUMN

Wandering aimlessly through the trees
So peaceful
Only the rustling of leaves.

Turn around, looking a long way back
I can see my footprints
Like a pattern in the track.

Some withered leaves start to fall
And right in front of me
A hedgehog crawls.

I watch its slow and graceful gait
As it shuffles through the fallen leaves
Is it searching for its mate?

On I walk quite undisturbed
Listening for the song
From a passing bird.

Then I find a rippling brook
What pleasures will I find
When I stop to look?

There's water beetles, and little frogs
With starey eyes peeping out
From under sunken logs.

The leaves have turned from green to brown
Trees shedding their summer coats
As the leaves fall to the ground.

The sun sets in the autumn cold
Nature's time to sleep
But still a beauty to behold.

THE BOOKIE

Ye' wee stoater
A've won ten quid
On a greyhound
Ca'ed Sleekie Sid.

Did ye see him go?
Whit a race,
He left them a' staunin'
Goin' at that pace.

I'll hae another bet
Jist a quid
Whit dug tae choose?
Go agin wae Sleekie Sid.

Silly dug slipped and fell
Lost that one, but whit the hell.
I'll pit aw the money I hae left
On a bonnie dug ca'ed Nippy Nell.

Whit happened there, she stopped
Right in the middle o' the track?
I'm gonne see the Bookie
Tae get ma money back.

The bookie saes, "Hard luck, chum,
Go bet anither race".
He's grinnin' noo fae ear to ear
A' think I'll punch his face.

A've used up a' ma winnin's
An a' ma wages tae,
Crivins, noo am scared goin' hame,
Whit will the wifie say?

She hit ma arm wae the rollin' pin
Noo it's in a stookie,
It's true whit a'm always telt
Ye cannie beat the Bookie.

MITHER'S DAY

It's Mither's Day the morrow
A've only wan an six,
She'd definitely no appreciate
A bag o' kindlin' sticks.

A've looked in a' the windaes
A'm in an awfie state
The cheapest bunch o' flooers
In the florist is wan an eight.

A git ma mind tae thinkin'
A way tae improvise
So a can gie ma mammy
A Mither's Day surprise.

So a picked a bunch o' daffies
Then she gied me dog's abuse
Cause a goat them in the gerdin
O' oor next door neighbour's hoose.

THE LAMPLIGHTER

The streets are dark and gloomy
People behind windows, curtains drawn tight
While others are still out walking
In the stillness of the night.

Then a stranger appears in the darkness
In the distance you hear him whistling
And just the faintest sound of footsteps
Can be heard if you're really listening.

The footsteps cease just for a moment
In his hand, a stick, lifted high,
Then the faintest glimmer of light
Can be seen against the darkened sky.

He walks slowly, never hurries
This stranger no one knows.
Is he happy doing what he's doing
As each night he comes and goes?

Soon he passes by the doorway
And leaves the street light shining bright
Then shadows out from the darkness creep
And dance in the flickering light.

Does he go to sleep in the daytime
While everyone else is awake
Or just sit at home in the darkness
Waiting for another day to break?

You know he's always coming
When darkness falls at night,
He never passes any street
If there's still a lamp to light.

Someday he won't be needed
There will be another source of power
Then he'll be able to have a rest
At this ungodly hour.

WATCHING

What was it that stopped me
Stepping off the kerb,
Was it basic instinct
Or a voice I heard?

What is it that makes me wary
Of driving on a certain road
Then hearing of an accident,
Does my brain have a secret code?

What is it that makes me sense
That a friend's ill, somewhere or other
Then knowing that this friend has died,
Is it messages from my mother?

Is she watching down on me
Giving me a helping hand,
Or is it some other force
I cannot understand?

Do I have a guardian angel?
There's nothing I can see
But I have the strangest feeling
Someone's watching over me.

SHIPYARDS

Majestic, she was
Launched on the tide
Down the slipway
On the River Clyde,
Men standing
Tears in their eyes
Dwarfed
By its magnificent size,
Proud shipworkers
Caps in hand
Watched the Queen Mother
Listened to the band.
Fine words spoken
Thousands listened
As the majestic ship
In the sea, glistened.

Tradesmen, managers,
Man and boy
Thousands, the shipyards
Did employ,
Each man, skilled
Working class
But what happened
Alas!
No more work
Orders lost
Owners too greedy?
At what cost
Unemployment,
Poverty, shame,
Whatever happens
Never be the same

Look down now
On the River Clyde
There's no more ships
Launched on the tide.

LIFE, LIVE IT

When a hand's held out in friendship
Take it

When opportunity knocks
Risk it

If there's a challenge
Face it

When you're going in the wrong direction
Change it

In a bad relationship
Break it

When there's hope of happiness
Grasp it

You've only got one life
Live it.

THE LOSERS

Vandalise
Terrorise
Caught
Lot
Shut up
Locked up
Crime
Time
Years
Tears
Regret
Fret
Homeless
Friendless
Drugs
Mugs
Clever
Never
Knife
Life
Appealed

Repealed.

TEMPTATION

A packet of o' crisps
Can of coke
Nothin' else
'Cause a'm broke.
Pass a bakehoose
Whit a smell,
Steemin' hot pies
Cakes as well.
Look around
Nae wan there
Could a' take wan
Could a' dare?

Near the door
Lies a tray
Wae a selection
Oan display,
Lift short breed
An' eccles cake
Fresh cream sponge
Wi' chocolate flake.

Turn around
Whit dae a' see
Twa beat bobbies
Watchin' me!
Better run
Best be quick
No quick enough
I'm in the nick.

MY BRAIN

My brain tells me to "Waken up,
Come now rise and shine,"
I open up one bleary eye
Heavens, is that the time!

It's half past two in the morning
I tell my brain to sleep
But all I hear it saying is
Why don't you try counting sheep?

This doesn't work, I'm still awake,
It's almost half past four
I now can hear the milkman
Leaving the pintas at my door.

Very soon it's half past five
I'm staring at the wall,
The alarm is ringing in my ears
As out of bed I crawl.

I start my work at half past six
Now my brain thinks it's time to sleep
I think I'll call in sick today
As back into bed I creep.

How can I teach this brain of mine
To sleep right through the night
Then I would waken in the morning
Feeling wide awake and bright.

KOSOVO

Sleep little children
Eyes closed tight
Have happy dreams
All through the night.

Bombs exploding
All around,
Hiding in shelters
Under ground,

Bullets flying
Overhead
People screaming
Others dead.

Sleep little children
For this last night
In the morning
We take flight.

Peace is coming
Soon we pray
In the mean time
We cannot stay.

The morn awakens
We cannot tarry
Lift possessions
All you can carry.

Outside all is quiet
Everyone flees
To join the hordes
Of refugees.

BAD DAY

I had a really bad day
Which started when I got up
I went to make a cup of tea
And broke my only cup.

I went to put my socks on
But couldn't find a pair
I put a sock on one foot
And left the other bare.

I tore my brand new jacket
So went to get some thread
Tripped over my old slippers
And fell upon my head.

I was standing on the pavement
My head still in a muddle
Went to go across the road
And fell into a puddle.

Standing in the post office
Waiting to buy a stamp
When the police came and threw me out
They thought I was a tramp.

So I decided I would go home
How could this happen to me
I went to open my front door
Had lost the ruddy key!

BANKRUPT, SO WHAT

I'm a bankrupt, so what?
It's not an infectious disease
Do people think it's something you catch
When you're out with friends and you sneeze?

My "friends" used to call me on Fridays
And ask me to go to the pub
Now there's only one person goes with me
All I get from the rest is a snub.

I'm a bankrupt, but I'm not invisible,
These "friends" walk past me in the street
They ignore all my telephone calls
And don't reply when I ask "Can we meet?"

I used to have pots of money
Had "friends" all around by the score,
Bar one, no one's offered to help me
My so called "good friends" are no more.

They loved when I bought them all presents
And took them for weekends to the sea
Now they've all vanished into thin air
Except one, who's standing by me.

I'm a bankrupt, but it won't be forever,
It's just another little hiccup in life
I'll make it with the help of my one friend
And that one good friend is my wife.

When I start climbing back up the ladder
I won't be splashing money all around
I'll remember what bankruptcy taught me
And keep my feet firmly down on the ground.

Real friends don't care if you're wealthy
Or if you're poor and don't have a lot,
They'll stand by you through all your troubles
True friendship can never be bought.

SMALL SIZE EIGHT

You've got to make it
You've got to try
Come on now mum,
Never say die.

Look, stretch your arms
Your right one round
Then the left one
Turn around,

Just bend a little
Then straighten up,
Right now, mum,
Try to zip up.

Dad's waiting on you
Breathe in tight
Hold in your tummy
With all your might.

Come on mum,
One more try
Hold your breath
Please don't sigh.

There, we've done it
You were great,
Getting a size fourteen
Into a small size eight.

KEEPING FIT

I bought a brand new tracksuit
And a pair of trainers too,
Joined the local sports club
To see what I could do.

I started on the tread mill
A walking pace at first
Stopped after just three minutes
'Cause I was dying of thirst.

I thought I'd try the bicycle
As exercise number two,
I had to stop again
To pay a visit to the loo.

The rowing machine looked easy
So I started working out on that
Painful on the knees it was
Gave up and rested on the mat.

Watched others lifting weights
I thought this'll do the trick
But after only six lifts
I was feeling rather sick.

I've decided the best way to keep fit
That isn't such a slog
Is to pack up my training gear
Go home and walk the dog.

FIELD OF RAPESEED

Likened to a soft yellow shawl blowing in the
    breeze
The field of rapeseed flowers is sheltered by a
    row of green fir trees,
High above, the summer sun shines down and
    warms the golden flowers
Then they're cooled in the evening by a
    sprinkling of light showers.

Take a step up on the stile and look over the
    field in wonder
To where the golden yellow hue meets the
    blue sky over yonder,
The colours mingle, the greens, the blues, the
    golds,
The beauty, the scent of nature before your
    eyes unfolds.

Dream of transporting this beauty to make a
    summer bower
Of golden yellow rapeseed retained forever
    in full flower,
Under which you can rest or quietly read a
    book
Or listen to the sound of a nearby rippling
    brook.

Take one long last look before you walk away
Cherish in your memory the pleasure of this
    day,
Seeing the farmer now standing with his hand
    upon the gate
He's come to harvest the rapeseed before it
    gets too late.

He looks at you and nods, then smiles a
    knowing smile
As if he knows you dreamed while standing
    on his stile,
He's stood where you stood taking pleasure
    from his land
At this crop of golden rapeseed that was sown
    by his own hand.

AULD STOOR SOOKER

Get oot the auld stoor sooker
'Cause friens are comin' tae visit
"Which cupboard is it in?
C'mon noo hen, where is it?"

Maggie brings it oot
Fae the cupboard unner the stairs,
Plugs it in, then gits started
Cleanin' aw the flairs.

The stoor sooker's awfie noisy
As it catches oan a rug
"Watch whit yer daen, hen
Ye micht sook up the dug"

Sometimes wae thae auld sookers
There's mair stoor comin' oot than in,
A' think it's time this stoor sooker
Gets dumped intae the bin.

"There's a stoor sooker oot withoot a bag
A' hear it's the latest invention,"
Maggie asked if we're getting wan,
A' tell her, "I've nae intention."

Mind ye, oor stoor sooker's had it
Cleanin' it oot is awfie messy.
I'll jist buy a bran new Dyson
An gie this yin tae Aunty Jessie.

GOAN GREY

There's nae way I'm goan grey
I'm gonna buy a tint,
Whit colour wid ye like me tae be?
C'mon noo, gies a hint.

A' think a'll go strawberry blonde
Or an auburn or dark red,
Or maybe a light chestnut
Is the colour a'll pick instead.

A' look at aw the colours
In boxes oan the shelf
At least a'm gonnie pick the wan
A' want tae dae myself.

At home a' pit the gloves oan
Follow the instructions tae the letter,
Once a' git rid o' aw this grey
A'll feel a million times better.

A' leave it oan fur therty minutes
An then a' rinse it oot
A' look masel in the mirror
Then pray that naebody's aboot.

The colour's run aw doon ma face
An ma hairs bricht orange and streaky
Ma daughter keeks her heid roon the door
An' screams, she thinks it's freaky.

She saes, "Oh maw, whit huv ye dun?
Yer no meant tae colour yer face,
Ye look like ye're dressed fur hallowe'en
As somewan fae ooter space."

A' wash and wash an it'll no come oot
Ma man tries to gie me solace,
By saying a' jist look like Mel Gibson did
When he played the pert o' William Wallace.

REALLY SWANKY

Ye'r werin' a kilt tae the waddin'
Ye want tae look really swanky,
Och, yer far too tall and lanky.

Yer legs are too skinny
An look at thae knees
Crivins, ye'd blaw ower in a breeze.

Turn roon 'til a hae a look,
Ye have'nae even goat a backside
The kilt aff yer hips'll just slide.

There's nae way yer sox'll stae up
An when ye pit in yer skean dhu
It'll likely faw doon tae yer shoe,

An hoo can say ye'r a Scotsman
Cause ye canny go withoot breeks
An let everywan see thae white cheeks.

Ye think a' the lassies'll fancy ye
If ye arrive dressed up like Braveheart,
Ye dinna look like Mel Gibson fur a start.

Jist pit oan yer guid suit and new tie
An a' promise ye'll still look really swanky
Even though ye're sae tall and sae lanky.

WHY DOES HE BEAT ME?

Love is tender
Love is caring
Love is sharing
Why then, does he beat me?

He opens the door
I smile at him
Then on a whim
He beats me.

I cook his meals
The best there is
He shouts "What's this!"
Then he beats me.

Then in the night
I try to please
He says I tease
Then again he beats me.

Love is tender
Love is caring
Love is sharing
Why then, does he beat me?

Police at the door
Husband's dead
A tear I shed
But I'll never know why he beat me.

THE OLD OAK SIDEBOARD

There's an old oak sideboard
standing in the hall
Hardly seen in the dark
against a gloomy unlit wall.

What treasures did it hold,
What memories held inside
Of generations past,
What secrets did it hide?

Maybe the drawers held letters
Sent by a soldier far away
Pledging lasting love and devotion
Promising to come home again some day.

In the cupboards there'd be linen
Given to the newly weds
And lace covered pillow cases
On which they laid their heads.

This old oak sideboard
More than a hundred years old,
What changes it had seen
As each year started to unfold.

Perhaps it held a dinner service
And cutlery gleaming bright
That graced the dinner table
When guests gathered for the night.

Now it's standing empty
Against that old dark wall
But still it's polished lovingly
While it stands there in the hall.

It belonged to my old grandmother
And now it's gifted down to me,
I'll take very good care of it
It's an heirloom now you see.

Its drawers will soon be full again
I'll fill them up with pleasure,
Of little gifts bestowed on me
The ones I'll always treasure.

I'll leave little notes inside the drawers
For my grandchildren, one day to see,
And they'll know the old oak sideboard
Held sweet memories of me.

THE PIANO PLAYER

Every day he practised
And every night he played
Anything from rock and pop
From jazz to Moonlight Serenade.

He's always the main attraction
At every party or event
He plays anywhere when asked
Even at the party in a tent.

The children love his melodies
When he entertains at local fairs
Especially the rousing tunes he plays
As they race round musical chairs.

On a Friday in the Old Folks' Home
There's no talking, not a sound,
Everyone is listening to ballads and old Scots
songs
Reliving memories, feet tapping on the ground.

At weddings, when he's invited
There's always volunteers to sing,
An odd tear is spotted in some folk's eyes
When he plays She Wears My Ring.

He's still playing the piano
Never earning much for a living
He says he gets payment enough
From all the pleasure he is giving.

But tonight we're paying a tribute
From old and young alike
To the piano player now in the Old Folks' Home
We've only ever known as Mike.

FRIENDSHIP

Stop thinking about what you're saying
And start saying what you think
Friends give you their opinions
Without even a blink.

You're always cautious
Not to offend
So you end up being dishonest
Even to a friend.

If they don't like your boyfriend
They soon let you know
Don't pretend you like theirs
If you don't, say so.

How many times have they said
They don't like how you've done your hair?
Now it's time to even the odds
Let's see just how much they care.

You always pretend not to be hurt
When others are being outspoken
You suppress your unhappiness
So that a friendship isn't broken.

Honesty between friends is right
So long as it isn't sarcasm,
Jealousy is sometimes a motive
And creates between friends a chasm.

Let friends always be truthful
And have each other's best interests at heart
You can learn much by being honest
And that's when a real friendship can start.

ONE TOO MANY

I'm sitting in the garden having a drink
After four glasses of champagne, I'm feeling in
    the pink,
Instead of ten rose bushes I seem to have
    twenty-two
I think I'll have a wild life park before I'm
    through.

The two squirrels have multiplied to eight
My garden's now a grand estate
My pond is now a swimming pool
And the garden table is full
Of champagne, and caviar
And wonderful delicacies in a jar,
For entertaining Royaltee
A huge marquee there will have to be.

I don't think I'll have another drink
As I'm no longer feeling in the pink,
My head is spinning round and round
I think I'm going to hit the ground.

Pink elephants are flying by
As I lie looking at the sky
And I'll have to go and spend a penny
Cause I've definitely had one drink too many.

ROOM FU' O'FOLK

Och my, I've never laughed sae much
The tears are runnin' doon ma cheeks
An a' jist keep laughin' an laughin'
'Till am nearly wettin' ma breeks.
Naebody else has seen anything funny,
Naebody sees the joke
An a'm the only wan laughin'
In a room that's fu o' folk.
It's jist that a've seen a man runnin'
Tae the loo as if he's in a race
When he trips on a loose piece o' carpet
An faws doon richt ontae his face.
He looks roon tae see if anywan's lookin'
An the only wan lookin' is me
His eyes catch me staunin' here grinnin'
As oot o' the room he dis flee.
A stert laughin' at his predicament
There's naebody else tae share the joke
An that's why I'm laughin' sae hearty
By ma'sel in a room fu o' folk.

WIN ONE, LOSE ONE

I've not paid the bills
I've not paid the rent
All my money has been spent,

There's little food inside my fridge
The cupboard's almost bare
I need some money, but from where?

The piggy bank is empty
No coins down the settee
I'm skint, poor worthless me.

Then in an old shirt pocket
I find a one pound note
I rush out without putting on my coat:

A pound of mince, a steak pie
Something nice for tea?
No, I'll spend the pound on me.

A lottery kiosk, I'll take a chance
I'll do without the food
'Cause I'm feeling in a really lucky mood.

Saturday night draw comes round
Six, ten, twenty, twenty-four
I only need two more!

Thirty-six and forty-two
That's the six numbers that I chose
I knew I couldn't lose.

I search my pockets, every one
In which drawer did I stick it?
Dear God, I've lost the bloomin' ticket!

THE STAG

Silhouetted against the moonlit sky
As the sun recedes behind the hill
The proud stag stands, antlers high
In the late evening when all is still.

Lifting his head upwards, he listens
Then lets out a resounding roar,
Birds take flight from all around
As into the twilight night they soar.

His hinds respond to their master's call
And move cautiously up the track,
The stag moves off, turning round
To check they're following at his back.

Still silhouetted against the sky
The stag is unaware of danger
His instinct is to lead his herd
He's unaware of a stalking stranger.

The hunter lifts his rifle, taking aim,
Through telescopic sights, at the stag's head
One single shot echoes through the hills
The magnificent stag is dead.

The hinds in panic run for cover
When they see their leader fall
As the hunter goes home happily
With a trophy for his wall.

STOPPING SMOKING

Eating sweeties
Chewing gum
Bad tempered
Looking glum
Biting finger nails
Pacing the floor
Sighing deeply
Stare at the door
Hands now sweating
Even shaking
Achievement
In the making
Fifteen minutes
Then thirty
Getting irate
Even shirty
Watch the clock
Seconds tick
Fifty minutes
Feeling sick
Keep going
One hour passed
I've stopped smoking
AT LAST!

DROPLETS OF RAIN

Little droplets of rain from overhanging trees
Slip slowly down to the tip of the leaves
Then, as if hanging on with all their might
They loosen their grasp and give up the fight
And plunge into the puddles below.

Try to imagine their fall in slow motion
Little droplets of rain falling into an ocean
Then splashing into the depths down below
Little waves from the impact start to flow
Rising and ebbing like the tide.

But we cannot see slow motion with our eyes
Rain comes down all at once from the skies
As the puddles spread further over the mud
They join together to create a flood
On the country road.

When the rain ceases the flood starts to recede
And on the drowned little insects, birds start
    to feed
Where the puddle has dried out in the sun
The insects' short life is now done
And the downpour is over.

Still hanging on to the tip of some leaves
Odd little droplets of rain remain on the trees
They slip off, no puddle now on which to land
I gently catch the last one in the palm of my
    hand
Before I let it fall.

MISSED THE BUS

I see my bus standing at the bus stop
So I start to run to catch it
The driver sees me in his mirror
Drives off - I nearly have a fit.

I keep running past the stop
So that I don't look like a fool
The bus is at the next stop
I'll catch it this time - Real Cool!

No - off it speeds again
So I have to keep running
As everybody's watching
I'll get it this time - I'll be cunning.

The bus is stopped again
At a red traffic light
Driver laughing, can't get on,
He's got the doors shut - tight.

I keep on running to prove the point
That I can catch this bus
I'll take the smile off the driver's face
Missed it again - I curse.

Take a rest to get a second wind
He won't be smiling when we meet,
I didn't realise I'd run so far
Until I'd ran right past my street.

STAYIN' AT HAME

The neighbours are gaun tae France
But cannie speak the lingo
Cousin Bella's gaun to Ibiza
But a'm gaun tae the bingo.

Ma frien's say they've spent twa grand
Oan a Mediterranean cruise,
They get sea sick gaun tae Rothsey
It's no the holiday a'd choose.

The folk doon the street are gaun to Mexico
They'll buy big hats just like a gringo,
But a've goat ma cerry out
An money fur ma bingo.

The're back awe sunburnt an seek
An' as skint as an auld church moose,
While a've just won ten grand
At the Mecca when a ca'ed full hoose.

Stayin' at hame's nae sae bad
Wi ma bingo and ma bevvy
While they come trudgin' hame wi duty free
Payin excess caus' their case's too heavy.

THE WILLOW TREE

I'm standing under the willow tree
Where we sat together in the sun
Now she's buried at this favourite spot
Where she used to play and run.

Her ears would pick up when I called her
She knew when we were going for a walk
Or when it was time for her dinner,
Sometimes I just wanted to clap her and talk.

When I was sad I'd sit beside her
Under the willow tree enjoying the breeze,
She'd nuzzle her head on my lap
As we listened to the rustle of the leaves.

The willow tree was our sanctuary
Where we could leave the world behind
And she always felt safe when we sat there
Especially when she got old and blind.

She was my companion for seventeen years
And now she lies forever under the willow tree
She'll be remembered, Shuna my dog,
As the most wonderful friend to me.

OPT OUT

Look forward, don't look back,
There's no way to back track
What you've done in the past
Is gone now, at last.
You can now look ahead
Plan for the future instead
Set a target, get a goal
Look into your innermost soul.

Go by your instinct
And really think
Of what you really want to do
What is the real you?
You've lived a life of stress
And ended up a mess,

You've had money to buy many things
Fancy house, car, diamond rings,
But never contentment, inner peace,
Work pressures never seemed to cease.

The more you have, the more you want,
Your worldly possessions you did flaunt
But they didn't bring you happiness
No, I must confess.
Opt out from this rat race
Take living at a leisurely pace.

A quiet island retreat
Warm sea in which I soak my feet
Living from the fruits of the land
Feeling my feet sink into warm sand,
No income, a wooden shack,
But I'm looking forward, not back
I've become so content
Living in the Bahamas in a tent.

WHAT I'D GIVE

It's my birthday tomorrow
And I'll be all alone
But at half past three
My daughter will phone.

I haven't seen her for ten years
She lives five miles away
She never comes to visit
And I'm never invited to stay.

She's done well for herself,
Married a professional man
And has two children
Who've never seen their gran.

They're educated at private school
And live in a fancy estate,
Probably are served their dinner
On a fancy china plate.

While I still stay in an old house,
Really it's a tenement flat
I'm obviously an embarrassment
And that's that.

But what I'd give just to meet them
I'd bake them scones for afternoon tea
And to hear my daughter's voice as I used to
Shouting "Happy Birthday, mum, it's me."

THE MOBILE PHONE

The guy in front's combing his hair
And talking into a mobile phone
He takes a bend far too fast
And drives into a wall of stone.

He scrambles out, thankfully unhurt
But his clothes are in a state
All he keeps saying as he staggers about
Is, "Where's ma mobile phone, a'm late",

His car, a new Mondeo, is lying in a heap,
The traffic's queuing up for miles
But searching through the wreckage
He finds his mobile phone and smiles.

Are you going to phone the police?
There's now a traffic jam right here
But he doesn't have the time right now
As he lifts the phone up to his ear.

"The car can be repaired," he says,
"An a' can always get a new suit,
But no havin' a mobile phone
Is somethin a' cannie dae withoot."

He ignores all the irate drivers
'Till one approaches without a sound
And taking the mobile phone from his hand
Scrunches it hard into the ground.

AUNTY BETTY

A've been goan tae ma Aunty Betty's
Fur ma dinner since a' wis a wean
Doon tae Lochwinnoch
Wance a month oan the train.

A git hame made soup,
Crusty broon bread, fae the local baker,
Curried chicken in a Homepride sauce
Wi' pepper oot the salt shaker.

Tinned peas, carrots an' new potatoes,
Hame made apple pie an' ice cream,
Then in front o' a roarin' fire
After Eights an coffee wae cream.

Her menu never changes
It widnae if she could
It's the meal we a' look forward tae
Goan tae Aunty Betty's is really good.

A' meet a' ma other cousins
An we pit the world tae right
Wae a' oor discussions
That go oan intae the night.

A' love ma Aunty Betty
An every meal's a winner
'Cause she keeps the family a' the gither
When we sit doon tae oor curried chicken
        dinner.

THINK TWICE

The loch is deep, deep
It's also cold, so cold,
I want to go to sleep, sleep.

My arms are in a cramp, cramp
Can't move my legs
My clothing feels damp, damp.

Water's going over my chin
Sinking, sinking
My chances are slim, slim.

Legs feel like lead, lead
Slipping away
Soon I'll be dead, dead.

My mind is drifting, drifting
Becoming oblivious
Someone's lifting, lifting.

Lying flat, voices loud, loud
Wrapped in a blanket
See a crowd, crowd.

Into freezing water they braved
To rescue me
Saved, saved.

Nearly paid the ultimate price
Ignored the warnings
Next time, think twice.

THAT SECRET

I can't tell you what I've done
I'm so full of shame.
What can I say
There's no one else to blame.

A friend told me a secret
Asked me not to tell
But I couldn't keep it to myself
So I told another friend as well.

Before I knew it, it was all around
The person not meant to hear, did,
Now her marriage is on the rocks
Because out of my stupid mouth words slid.

Every person who was told
Exaggerated the story quite a lot
Now it's out of all proportion
And I'm really in a spot.

Is it my fault for sharing a secret
Or my friend's for telling me first?
We both broke a confidence
Which one of us is the worst.

I regret now not keeping that secret
I should have kept my mouth shut
Because a lot of people along the way
Got really, really hurt.

At the time I felt really smug
Now I've learned the story wasn't true
Even worse than that
The lies just grew and grew.

Now I'm full of remorse and guilt
For spreading a malicious lie
Perhaps I'll be forgiven
Eventually, as time goes by.

I WANT TO HAVE THE POWER

I want to have the power
To stop wars and starvation
To make all people feel friendship
From nation to nation.

I want to have the power
To cure all the diseases
From the most serious of illnesses
To the simplest of sneezes.

I want to have the power
To make rains fall on arid land
And governments to give crops to grow
On fertile ground that once was sand.

I want to have the power
To stop every earthquake and flood
And to stop all the bombing that causes
The spilling of innocent blood.

I want to have the power
To make the world a happier place
That we can all be content in
And stop spending billions on the arms race.

I want to have the power
To make all people of the world stand
To look on each other as equals
And go into the future hand in hand.

I wish I had the power
But all I can do is pray
That future governments learn to work together
To make this world a better place in which to
stay.

GLOBAL WARMING

There's no snow at Christmas
The sun starts to shine
Just like it does in the summertime;

It doesn't rain very often
The rivers are dry
But the tides seem to be rising ever so high.

We've got mosquitoes now
And sharks in our seas
Unknown viruses coming in on the breeze;

Spring, summer, autumn and winter
All blend together
Whatever has happened to our weather?

The scientists told us
This would happen someday
Although we thought it was still years away;

The icebergs are melting
There's no glaciers forming
It's here, as we feared, GLOBAL WARMING.

CLOUDS

Watching the gathering of the clouds
Covering the sun like dark grey shrouds
Blocking out the sun's rays
Often for days and days,
Shielding the earth from its heat
Keeping the warmth from our feet,
Lack of sunshine slows the growth of the grain
But the clouds supply us with essential rain.

The clouds bring darkness when there's thunder
Lightning can strike while we slumber,
The downpour of rain from the clouds in the sky
Creates floods in the fields where cattle lie,
But in the blessed morn
Look up from where the rain has flattened the
    corn
And watch the sun come out on a brand new
    day
As, for a time, the clouds stay away.

THE DAISY CHAIN

I'm going to make a daisy chain
Before he mows the lawn
'Cause he'll soon cut the heads off
And all the daisies will be gone.

He calls them weeds and digs them out
They're not welcome in his lawn,
But I'm going to pick them all
And when he gets here they'll be gone.

I've made a great big daisy chain
And I've crept into his shed
While he's having his afternoon nap
I'll decorate his head.

When he awakens I'll tell my dad
He's a king wearing a daisy crown,
And he looks very handsome
When he wears a smile not a frown.

I'll show him how pretty daisies are
And ask him to let them grow in his lawn,
But I know the next time he cuts his grass
The daisies will soon be gone.

A BOWL OF FRUIT

An apple, banana, grapes and a pear
Sit in a bowl on a locker beside a faded
    plastic chair

The fruit's inedible, overripe, almost rotten
It's been there for weeks lying forgotten.

The man in the hospital bed lies dying
The old lady sitting in the plastic chair is crying,

She holds the man's frail hand, giving it heat
As the old man's heart struggles to beat.

Soon, it's all over the old lady says her last
    goodbyes
As she wipes the last tear from her bloodshot
    eyes,

She lifts the bowl of fruit, such a waste, such a
    sin,
Leaving the ward she sadly drops the bowl of
    fruit in the bin.

THE CONGREGATION

The minister is standing in the pulpit preaching
From one of the Gospels he is teaching
The Congregation.

He spouts about God's wrath
And how to honour the Sabbath
To the Congregation.

Now bow your heads and pray
Bless us all, this day,
Says the Congregation.

Sitting on wooden benches, are the poor and
    the wealthy
Mixing with the sick and the healthy
Making up this Congregation.

Adhere to the ten Commandments,
The minister laments,
God bless the Congregation.

A hymn is sung, Communion taken
The dozing elderly start to waken
From within the Congregation.

The sermon is over, the service done
The benches are emptied, one by one,
By the Congregation.

They attend this church faithfully each Sunday
But revert to being sinners come Monday,
Does this Congregation.

This special service is held in a jail
Where each prisoner's life is a different tale
This unusual Congregation.

Will they learn to heed the gospel and repent?
Will society relent
And forgive this Congregation?

THE DARTS MATCH

A've hurt ma back
It's awfie sair
A' fell when runnin'
Doon the stair.

A' need a doctor
Cae him oot
Ma leg's sair tae
An so's ma foot.

Ma heid is thumpin'
Ma hauns are shakin'
Is that a cup o' tea
Ye're makin'?

A' cannie walk
Can ye no see
This awfie pain
Is cripplin' me.

A'm stayin' aff work
'Cause a'm no fit
A' need tae staun'
A' cannie sit.

Rab's at the door
They're short o' a player
Ma back's feelin'
No sae sair.

It's the darts final
Doon the local pub,
Get oot the Ralgex
Gie ma back a rub.

A' ken a' cannie sit
But the pub's no far
An a, can staun,
Haudin' ontae the bar.

A' cannie let the team doon
It's a darts match efter awe
An efter a few beers
A'll forget a' hud a faw.

AS GUID AS NEW

Here Hen, here's yer new coat,
Weel, it's as good as new
A' bought it at the jumble sale
A' hud the choice o' quite a few.

Look, the linin's no even stained
Wae unner erm swettin',
It must hae belanged tae somewan posh
Whit's the bettin'.

It's goat a designer tag oan
Look it's made by Next
Naw, it disnae mean it's next in line
An noo the zip's needin' fixed.

A ken it's hingin' doon tae yer feet
But it's still as guid as new,
An long styles are aw the fashion
An it's sitch a bonnie shade o' blue.

Stop greetin', I'll tak it in a bit
I'll mak it intae a nice size ten,
Och I'll even git it dry cleaned
Ye'll look awfie bonnie in it, hen.

Naebody'll ken it's second hand
By the time a'm feenished wae it
Ye'll git loads o' wolf whistles
Wance a' mak it a really guid fit.

There, aw dun, whit a stunner
The boys'll be aw waitin' in a queue
To date ma wee smasher
Werrin' a coat that's guid as new.

CANDLE LIGHT

Candle light
Shining bright
Bottle of wine
Two people dine
Holding hands
Making plans
Sparkling ring
What will life bring?
Joy, sorrow?
Beg or borrow?
Children, happiness?
Barren, childless?
Health?
Wealth?
The path is unknown
Seeds are sown
In the candlelight
Shining bright.

SKINT KNEE

Ye've skint yer knee
Let's see
It's no sae bad
Dinna look sae sad.

How did ye fa?
Ye fell aff the wa',
Whit were ye daen'
When ye were playin'?

Wipe yer ee
Gimme yer knee
I'll pit oan a plaster
It's no a disaster.

There's nae blood
Jist mud
Ye can look doon
It'll be better soon.

Noo dinna greet
I'll gee ye a sweet,
Hiv twa mair
Guid, it's no sae sair.

It's great whit a sweet'l dae
Awa back oot an play,
Tak oot yer fitba
An' stae off the wa'.

MY COMPANIONS

My floor's never clean
The carpet's are mucky
But I still think
I'm very lucky
To have two companions
Two Springer Spaniel dogs
Who come with me to the woods
Each day when I'm chopping up logs.
They've got boundless energy
As they race to and fro
I never get bored
Watching them go
Chasing rabbits
That they never catch
For speed
They've met their match.

At the end of the day
When the logs are all stacked
In front of the fire
They flop, totally whacked
All tuckered out
Completely beat
They lie together
Enjoying the heat.
It's here they'll stay
When I go off to bed
They're perfectly content
After being fed
Then first thing in the morning
At the door they will be
Waiting patiently
Just for me.

EARLY WINTER SNOW

The first early snow of winter sends
Rabbits scurrying into their burrows,
The stag and his hinds make haste
Into the forest next to where the river bends.

Cattle huddle together in the corner of the field
While sheep flock to shelter beneath hedgerows,
The animals hide in any corner that gives protection
As from the icy snow they try to shield.

Foxes in dens with their cubs
Are too scared to venture in search of food,
Hinds encourage the fawns to suckle
While they feed on the tips of shrubs.

The snow falls heavier day by day
Until only the tops of gate posts can be seen,
The farmer loads the trailer of his tractor
Then battles through drifts with bundles of hay.

Not days, but weeks go by
Before the snows relent,
Then gently a slow thaw starts, the snows melt
When the sun comes out in a clearing sky.

The fully grown animals who survived on the hillside
Wander out of their shelter to search for food
Alas, when the snows melt finally away
The youngest and the frailest have not survived.

The farmer's saddened by the animal's plight
As he surveys the dead lying on the hillside
And he curses the arrival of the early winter snow
And knows he'll never get used to this heart
    breaking sight.

COUNTING THE DAYS

I'm counting the days 'till I'm sixty
When I'll be able to retire
I'll get my bus pass and free prescriptions
And in cold mornings I'll sit by the fire.

No more getting out of bed at six thirty
To get to the factory by seven,
I'll lie in bed until eight thirty
Thinking that I'm in seventh heaven.

I know I won't have as much money
But my pension will have to suffice
Going on holiday at any time in the winter
Is going to be really quite nice.

I'll spend the afternoon with my sister
And some mornings I'll go for a swim
Then if I'm feeling really energetic
I'll go for a workout at the gym.

I know I won't find life boring
There's so many places I'm longing to see
And I'll have my friends for company
Because they'll be retiring like me.

I'm counting the days 'till I'm sixty
When I'm definitely going to retire
And with all of the plans that I'm making
I won't have the time to sit by the fire.

BOWL O' SCOTCH BROTH

A' gie ma weans a bowl o' Scotch Broth
That's fu o' lentils an barley,
Jimmy's growin' awfie big
But ye should see the height o' Charlie.

A' mak the soup jist like ma mither did
An' awe the generations gone afore
An' walkin' in the close at night
The smell o' it's waftin' oot the door.

Oor Charlie his it fur his breakfast
An' hus mair when he comes in fur tea
He's still only ten years auld
But he's nearly as big as me.

The soup pot's always oan the stove
An awebody's mair than welcome
To git the ladle oot the pot
An' fill a bowl an' hae some.

Crusty breed an hame made broth
Is a supper fit fur a king
Ye dinna need onything else tae eat
Naw, no anither thing.

Guid ham stock an lots o' veg
An' plenty lentils an barley
Then hae a bowl of hame made Scotch Broth
An ye'll grow up big and strong like Charlie.

A VISIT

I saw her standing in the corner of the room
Silent, motionless, staring,
I moved closer till our eyes met
Then I recognised the clothes she was wearing,
On closer inspection
Her face was familiar too
She didn't speak, silent, still
That face, was a face I knew
But how, that familiar face
I hadn't seen for years
The last time, I remember when we met
I shed so many tears
She was dying then, so long ago
The exact time I can't remember
But now, she stands in front of me
Smiling, so gently and so tender.
I blinked, then looked again and she was gone,
Was it an illusion, a shadow of light?
Or a ghost, the spirit of my friend
That paid me a visit in the night.

CHRISTMAS CHEER

It's Christmas time, an' a'm no jolly
So a didnae buy any holly
An' mistletoe, forget that
I'm no kissin' anywan, I'd feel a prat.

Christmas crackers, festive cheer
I'm no celebratin', nae fear,
Tell the weans tae mak less noise
An' go awa an' play wae their new toys.

Big fat turkey, Christmas pud
It's no daen ma cholestral any good,
Repeat films oan the telly
Weans stuffin' their faces wae ice cream an jelly.

Carol singers at the front door
Auld grandpa lets oot a loud snore,
Peace oan earth, weel there's nae peace in here
A'm awa doon tae the pub for a beer.

Walk intae the pub everywans singin'
Christmas bells fae the corner are ringin'
Roll oan Boxin' Day when everywan's oan a diet
An a git back tae work fur some peace an quiet.

THE GARDEN

We've got plastic gnomes in our garden
Some statues and a fountain,
If my husband had his way
We'd have a blooming mountain.

There's plants I've never heard of
That grow as big as trees
Four bee hives in the corner
For the little honey bees.

There's a pond that's for the goldfish
And a bird table, like a doll's house,
There's little logs and bags of nuts
For the squirrels and the odd field mouse.

Foxes come into our garden
To play around the bird bath and tubs,
Every kind of bird you can imagine
Lands on our fruit trees and shrubs.

There's bat boxes for the bats
And security lights everywhere,
All I'm waiting for him to bring home
Is a garden rocking chair.

There's a BBQ and garden tables
And a trellis for the clematis,
And the strongest metal creation
I haven't a clue what that is.

The garden's my husband's pride and joy
It's treated like a country estate
But the truth of the matter is
It's only twenty feet by twenty-eight.

PLASTERED

Climbing over the farm gate
I fell off and broke my wrist
I landed rather badly
So it got quite a twist.

Up to the A and E
At the local hospital
It was so busy
Just like a shopping mall.

My turn, X-ray first,
C'mon now dear,
Plaster on,
That was my greatest fear.

Plastered up to my elbow
Can't bend my arm
Wish I'd never gone
For a walk through the farm.

Can't fasten my bra
Or pull up my knickers
Or tie the laces
On my brand new red Kickers.

Husband thinks it funny
He's having the last laugh
'Cause he's got to help me
Out the bloomin' bath.

Just wait till I get my plaster off
I'll give him quite a shock
'Cause his head
Is going to get a knock

With a plaster cast that's covered
With umpteen autographs
An' when he's holding his head
I'll be the one that laughs.

SOCIAL DRINKING

I drink to be sociable, I drink to unwind
I drink with my friends, we're three of a kind.

I drink to be happy, I drink to forget
Any excuse and I'll drink for a bet.

I have a few too many before I go to bed
But it helps me forget the worries inside my head.

Drinking helps me dream of loving couples
    walking hand in hand
Walking barefoot together along a golden sand.

I dream of tree lined avenues, blossom trees
    in bloom
And beautiful vases of fresh flowers, brightening
    up my room.

The bad time's the following morning when
    I'm feeling really sick
And I have to run into the bathroom very very
    quick.

A hangover's what I have to suffer for my
    pleasure the night before
I have to run to the bathroom again before I
    go out the door.

I've decided no more gin, no more social
    drinking,
No more hangovers, that's what I'm really
    thinking.

I've been sober now, for really quite a while
I've even remembered, what it's like to smile.

I can see my life clearly now, not through a haze
I'm not living my life anymore in that
    constant daze.

And as for the dreams, now I'm out of the
    constant gloom
I'm sitting looking, at the vase of flowers,
    which brightens up my room.

LITTER

There's litter everywhere
On the pavements, on the streets
Leaving the cinema
You see litter left between the seats.

We've become a really careless nation
Who throw cigarette packets out of cars
Drop paper bags and lemonade bottles
Even glasses lifted from public bars.

Some parents seem to let their children
Drop all their litter at their feet
It doesn't matter what it is
Even a small paper off a sweet.

There's litter on our beaches
And all over the countryside
Do we not care about the impression we give?
Where is our national pride?

Teaching pride should start in the home
Surely our children we can educate
To take their litter home with them
Not leave our towns and cities in a state.

When litter bins are provided
You're meant to put your litter in
Not drop it anywhere you please
Put it in the bin.

We have a beautiful country
That attracts visitors from overseas
Show them we care about our country
Don't drop your litter, PLEASE.

THE PULLEY

Oor pulley runs the length o' the kitchen
An' it hings high above yer heid
If it draps doon when ye'r no lookin'
It could kill ye, stane deid.
When mither's dun aw the washin'
An' she's cerried it aw up the stair
The baskets heavy an' she's puffed oot
She draps the basket ontae the flair,
The pulley's let doon wae a thud
An' it's a' hauns tae help
If ye try tae git oot o' it
Mither'll gie yer heid a guid skelp.
The wet sheets git hung oan the pulley
An' if ye try tae duck unnerneath
Yer likely tae git a wet sheet
Smackin' ye richt back oan the teeth.
When the pulley's at last crammed fu'
It's hoisted richt back up tae the ceilin'
The thing noo weighs half a tun
The pain in yer erms leaves ye reelin'.
Ye hiv tae keep dookin' an' divin'
Unner the sheets that hiv been hingin' fur days
But efter the heat fae the fire's dried them oot
It's time tae hing up a' the claes.
It's great when it's the summertime
An' the claes are hung tae dry ootside
An' ye dinna need tae worry aboot
Getting hit wi' a swingin' pulley oan yer
    backside.

THE ROBIN

Wee robin
Wae it's red breast
Sat oan a branch
Fur a wee rest
Flappin' its wings
There it sang
Didnae sit
Very lang
Creepin' slowly
Unnerneath
Pounced, got the robin
In its teeth
Next door's
Big tom cat
Kilt the robin
An' that's that.

LANG TROOSERS

Maw, will ye buy me a pair o' lang troosers
At least wans that'll cover ma knees?
Even ma goose pimples are beginning tae
    freeze.

A've been wearin' these short troosers
Since a sterted goan tae the school,
Aye, maw, a' ken they're made o' pure wool.

At least the sheep's legs were always kept warm
Wae a woolly fleece attached tae its legs
Mine look like a pair o' frozen clothes pegs,

An a' ken ye let the seams oot
An they fit a richt here and there
But they're sae short, people a' stare.

Ma pals are awe wearin' lang troosers noo,
An aye maw a'm embarrassed being seen
Still wearin short troosers, at the age o' sixteen.

WEDDING PHOTOGRAPHS

Smile please
Say cheese
Hold it

Smile please
Say cheese
Hold it

Move here
Stand there
Hold it

Smile please
Say cheese
Hold it

Over there
Don't stare
Smile please

Bride and groom
More room
Smile please

Families now
Page boy, bow
Smile please

Smile please
Say cheese
Hold it

Second take
Cutting cake
Hold it

Stand together
End of tether
Smile please

Last one
Smile please
Say cheese

HOLD IT

DO I WANT

Do I want
Pension, credit card, double glazing?
The list is endless, quite amazing.

Do I want
Chairs re-covered, cruises, catalogues
Bathroom suites, kitchens, fires with logs?

Or do I want
Television, videos or a computer game
Just about anything that you can name?

Do I want
Fridges, freezers, wooden flooring
Power tools or machines for boring?

Do I want
Garden paving, shears to cut back trees
Or a hoover machine that sooks up leaves?

No, I don't want
Anything, anything at all,
Advertising leaflets are driving me up the wall.

What I really want
Is a shouting letter box
That shouts, 'No junk mail!' before the
postman knocks.

CHRISTMAS DAY

It's Christmas Day
Around the table I survey
My family whom I love so dearly
This Christmas day, it's very clearly
The happiest day of my year.

Sitting down to a wonderful spread
Soon we'll all be really well fed
On turkey, ham and Christmas pud
As this Christmas dinner is as it should
Be, full of festive cheer.

So I give thanks to my God above
For blessing me with so much love
I wish you all happiness and health
And with a little luck some extra wealth
May your future wishes be fulfilled
As I lift my glass of champagne, duly chilled
And wish you a Very Merry Christmas.